CHLOE *by* DESIGN

THE FIRST *Cut*

BY MARGARET GUREVICH

ILLUSTRATIONS & PHOTOS BY BROOKE HAGEL

STONE ARCH BOOKS™
a capstone imprint   www.capstonepub.com

Chloe by Design is published by Stone Arch Books
A Capstone Imprint
1710 Roe Crest Drive
North Mankato, Minnesota 56003
www.capstonepub.com

Library of Congress Cataloging-in-Publication Data
Gurevich, Margaret, author.
The first cut / by Margaret Gurevich ; illustrated by Brooke Hagel.
pages cm. -- (Chloe by design ; [2])

Summary: Both sixteen-year-old Chloe Montgomery and her long time
rival, Nina, have made it through the first round of the California Teen
Design Diva audition — but more rounds lie ahead and each round
promises to be more challenging than the one before.

ISBN 978-1-4342-9178-3 (hardcover) - ISBN 978-1-4965-0070-0 (eBook PDF)

1. Fashion design--Juvenile fiction. 2. Auditions--Juvenile fiction. 3.
Television game shows--Juvenile fiction. 4. Self-confidence--Juvenile
fiction. 5. Friendship--Juvenile fiction. 6. Santa Cruz (Calif.)--Juvenile
fiction. [1. Fashion design--Fiction. 2. Reality television programs--Fiction.
3. Competition (Psychology)--Fiction. 4. Friendship--Fiction. 5. Santa Cruz
(Calif.)--Fiction.] I. Hagel, Brooke, illustrator. II. Title.
PZ7.G98146Fi 2014
813.6--dc23
2013048156

Designer: Alison Thiele
Editor: Alison Deering

Photo Credits: Brooke Hagel, 20; Shutterstock/Andrekart Photography,
65 (top left), nito, 65 (bottom left), J.D.S, 65 (top right)

Artistic Elements: Shutterstock

Printed and bound in China.
10288R

Measure twice, cut once
or you won't make the cut.

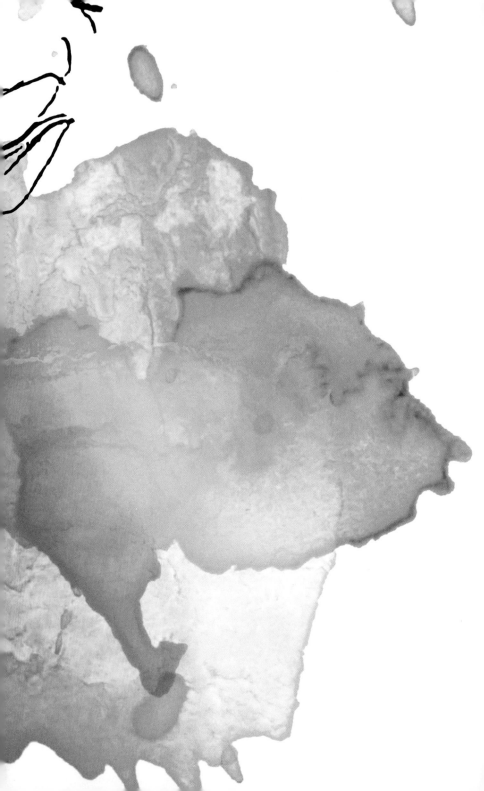

_1_

Well, it's official. Nina and I are celebrities. It figures
that when I finally get my big break — or at least a shot
at it — my number-one rival would be right there with
me. I've spent basically my whole life with Nina LeFleur
copying me, so why should this be any different?

The celebrity buzz started when we both made it
through the first round of the _Teen Design Diva_ auditions
last week. In the five days since the auditions, the local
papers have been calling nonstop about interviewing
us. One newspaper even started a blog called "The
Sweethearts of Santa Cruz" so they can keep everyone
updated about our progress in the competition.

I'm not sure what they're going to do if Nina and
I don't make it to New York City. (Probably start

another blog to chronicle our downfall.) Nina clearly isn't worried. The way she's acting — blowing kisses to anyone within two feet of her — you can tell *not* making it is *not* an option for her.

I wish I had some of Nina's confidence, but there are still have two more rounds of auditions to go. The second one is supposed to revolve around accessories, while the third one is some mystery rodeo challenge. No one seems to know exactly what the final challenge will entail, especially since the massive California Rodeo, which is held in Salinas, usually isn't held until the third week in July. I heard a rumor that they might be holding a special event to promote *Teen Design Diva* and increase the rodeo hype, but so far it's just that — a rumor.

I guess it makes sense for the local media to milk it for all it's worth now. If Nina and I do make it to New York City, everything will be taped and kept strictly under wraps. The new set of rules I got is very explicit about keeping everything hush-hush during the two weeks of taping.

"Like, OMG," says Alex in a high-pitched voice as she walks up to my locker on Friday after school. "Are you Chloe Montgomery? Like for real? Amazing fashion designer and future star of *Teen Design Diva*? Can I get your autograph?"

"Cut it out," I say, feeling myself blush. Alex has been getting a huge kick out of my newly minted celeb status. Not only does she get to laugh at my discomfort, but because we're usually joined at the hip, she also gets to enjoy all the perks without having to suffer any of the embarrassment.

"Aw, come on. You should be enjoying this a little more. Nina sure is," Alex says, nodding down the hallway. Sure enough, I turn and see Nina strutting toward us, fake smile firmly in place. A crowd of mini-Ninas trails adoringly behind her.

"Ugh. I can't deal with her right now," I mutter. Nina and I may have called a truce for the time being, but I still don't want to be BFFs. I'm sure she doesn't either, but the reporters who have been hounding us seem to want us to be friends rather than rivals, so she's playing that up for them. I just do my best not to grimace every time she hugs me.

"Chloeee!" Nina squeals as she runs to me. "How have you been, girl?" She leans in and air kisses me on both cheeks.

"Hey, Nina. You feeling ready for the next round?" I ask. The mini-Ninas immediately perk up. They love hearing about anything that has to do with the competition.

"Almost," says Nina, smiling. "There's an art fair tomorrow I'm planning to hit up for some inspiration. See you there?"

"Maybe," I say, keeping my answer vague. The truth is, Alex and I have been looking forward to the art fair all week, but I don't need to give Nina any more opportunities to steal my ideas.

"Cool," Nina says with a tight smile. She gives me a quick hug goodbye and motions for her posse to follow. They do, blowing air kisses to me as they go.

"I don't know how you put up with her," Alex says when they're gone. "She's so fake it makes me sick to my stomach."

"Yeah, tell me about it," I agree. "But I figure the competition will be at least slightly less painful this way."

I swing my backpack over my shoulder, and Alex and I head out the school doors. As soon as we're outside, a bright flash goes off. I shield my eyes and see three reporters, notepads and recorders ready. One of them excitedly motions to me. I groan and walk over to them. Nina is already there, arms moving animatedly as she tells some story.

It seems like my CC nickname — the one my best friend Alex created for me when I first heard about auditions — is changing once again. First it was

Cowardly Chloe, then Courageous Chloe. Celebrity Chloe, here I come.

* * *

The next day there's a slight breeze, and the temperature is in the mid-seventies — perfect weather for an art fair. There's nothing worse than looking for bargains under a sweltering sun while making sure beads of sweat don't ruin the very items you're trying to bargain for. Alex and I have been at the fair for an hour already, and we've barely scratched the surface. That could be because Alex keeps gravitating toward the food samples. Not that I'm protesting too hard — who turns down free chocolate?

"It's not just the free food that's slowing us down here," says Alex between bites. "Do you even know what you want to design?"

I pretend to be extremely interested in choosing a good chocolate sample so I don't have to answer right away. For the second round of auditions, I have to design an accessory that complements one of the three designs I created for the first round. The guidelines for that first challenge required each designer to create three designs that represented his or her personal style. I opted for a white dress with a cinched waist and full skirt, tuxedo leggings and a tunic, and a silk shift dress with an asymmetrical hemline — all designed to reflect my simple-chic design aesthetic.

Now the judges want us to demonstrate our versatility as designers and see if we can give an existing piece "new dimension." Alex knows I really have no idea what accessory I want to make yet. I haven't even decided which piece to accessorize! I've narrowed it down to the leggings-and-tunic ensemble or the first dress — there's no way I'm revisiting that silk disaster after the judges' comments. I can still hear Jasmine's words: "The stitching. Uh-uh. Not gonna fly."

"Not yet," I finally admit. "I want it to be just right. I'll know it when I see it." I try to sound confident, like that's how designers work. I'm really hoping it's true.

Alex shrugs her shoulders. "Doesn't matter to me. I could spend all day here," she says. "I love people watching, and I see rows and rows of food samples to keep me busy. Just don't try to play it off like it's my fault your hands are empty."

I laugh and give Alex a playful shove. She knows me too well. "If I don't blame you then I have to blame myself, and that's no fun."

Alex laughs too. "Tough to be you. Ooh, wait. Check out that booth over there," she says. She points across the aisle. "I can't tell exactly what they're selling, but it looks colorful. Come on."

I trail after Alex. When it comes to accessories, I tend to be a bit more liberal with color than I am with my wardrobe, which is usually full of neutrals. The right shade of a fiery tone can add spark to a bland top, and a funky metallic can add just enough pop to make an outfit really shine.

We arrive at the booth Alex spotted, and for a few seconds I just stand there admiring all the gorgeous jewelry. I browse the pendants on the table. The stones are all shades of orange and red and attached to antique chains. These pieces have an old-world feel to them, which is cool, but they won't work with my designs. The colors aren't right for me leggings and tunic, and the antique feel doesn't match the modern tone of either garment. We walk around more, but nothing on the table is exactly right.

"I need to have some sort of a plan," I tell Alex. "Otherwise I'm never going to be able to pick something. I'm going with the dress." I stare at my best friend expectantly, like she's supposed to jump up and down at the fact that I made a decision.

"Great, let's keep looking," says Alex.

"That's it?" I say. "No excitement about me finally making a choice?"

Alex laughs. "Oh, sorry. Let me give you the appropriate applause." She pretends her hands are a camera and starts snapping away. People walk around us. Some are amused, and others annoyed that we're in their way in an already crowded street.

"Stop," I mumble. Maybe I've gotten too used to the reporters fawning over my design decisions if I expected Alex to pat me on the back.

"Celebrity Chloe," says Alex, transforming her hands into a microphone and holding them up to my mouth, "can you please tell us about how you came to the decision to accessorize your dress instead of the leggings and tunic?"

Some people actually stop, realizing who I am. I want to fall through the ground. "Okay, okay, I get it. No more. Please." I shield my face and walk away from her through the crowd.

Alex runs after me, obviously not ready to let the joke go quite yet. I speed up, not watching where I'm going, and end up crashing into a table. When I look up, the boy I see makes me forget all about why I'm here in the first place.

"Oh, jeez. I'm so sorry," I say, gazing up into the boy's gorgeous green eyes. "I wasn't looking where I was going."

The mystery boy smiles at me, and when he does, I notice that he has a dimple in each cheek. "No harm done," he says, but I can see him rearranging a few of the pieces on the table. "Looked like you were a girl on a mission."

"She definitely is," Alex suddenly pipes up. I didn't even realize she was standing behind me. "Don't you know who she is?"

"Stop it, Alex," I hiss at her. Sometimes I could kill my best friend.

Mr. Green Eyes, however, looks amused. He raises his eyebrows. "I don't," he says to Alex. "But please do tell."

"You're looking at a contestant on *Teen Design Diva*," Alex says. "Just made it past the first round, which is why we're here. She needs inspiration for round two." She is having way too much fun embarrassing me, but I also know she's super proud of me.

Green Eyes looks impressed. "You're going to be on that show? That's awesome!"

I blush. "Well, not yet. I've only made it past the first round of auditions. We'll see what happens in round two. I have to design accessories to complement one of my existing designs."

"Well, I want to do my part to make sure you make it," he says. "I mean, imagine if you win. I can tell all my buddies at Parsons that I met you before you were famous."

This time, I can tell he's being silly. He winks at me, and I blush again. But, wait, did he just say Parsons? That's only my number-one dream school for fashion design. "How do you know about Parsons? Do you want to be a fashion designer too?" I ask.

"Not exactly," he says. "I'm studying fashion marketing there. My mom is the brains behind these pieces, but I'm her go-to on these travel missions. She likes to stay on the design end of things, and it's good practice for me." He reaches up to brush a strand of his dark hair from his eyes.

I force myself to stop staring at Green Eyes and focus on the jewelry and stones spread across the table. After all, that's what I'm here for. The pieces really are exquisite. If you look closely at the stones, you can see crystals reflected underneath. I can feel Green Eyes watching me as I study them.

"How about this?" he suggests, holding up a brass chain. At the end is something that looks like a little cage, and inside is a reddish-orange sphere with sharp edges. The red reflects out of the cage, casting streams of colored light on the table.

"It's cool," I say, "but I don't think it'll quite work. I'm supposed to be creating something, not buying it. And I think I need something a little shorter to keep the proportions in line for the dress I'm accessorizing. I'm leaning toward a statment necklace of some kind." I feel like I should apologize or something, but Green Eyes just looks thoughtful.

"I think I have the perfect pieces," he says. He ducks under the table, and I can hear him digging through a few boxes. When he finally comes up, he's holding a bunch of clear, crystal stones and metallic studs in a variety of shapes and sizes. The studs all have a cool, vintage look. As he moves his hand, the light hits the stones, making them sparkle.

I'm about to ask him why they aren't on the table with the others, but then I realize why. Each one has little pieces broken off or some other imperfection about it. But for my purposes they're perfect. They have just the right amount of distressing. I can already picture a cool statement necklace adding the perfect accent to the neckline of my dress. I can even use them on the shoulders of my dress or along the waistband to create an embellished belt.

"You were right," Alex says to me. "You'll know when you see it." Turning to Green Eyes, she adds, "You have a great eye for detail."

This time he's the one who blushes. "Thanks." He puts all the pieces in a shopping bag for me, then takes the cage necklace and puts it around my neck. "On me," he says.

I touch the necklace. "You don't have to do that," I tell him.

"The stones weren't something my mom could have sold anyway. She won't care. And the necklace . . . well, just wear it on the show," he says he says with a cute grin. "Mention my mom's designs, if you can." He hands me a card with the words "Jewels by Liesel" written on it in neat cursive.

I study the card carefully. The name of the line sounds so familiar. "I think I've heard of her," I say.

Green Eyes shrugs. "Yeah? It's possible." He grins, like he's keeping a secret. Maybe he thinks I'm just making that up to be nice.

"Well . . . thanks again," I say, stepping away from the table. I hold out my hand to shake goodbye, and Alex bursts out laughing. I don't know what possessed me to do that. I want to pull my hand back, but before I can, Green Eyes is holding it firmly.

"No problem," he says with a smile. "By the way, what's your name?"

"Um, it's Chloe," I reply. Our hands are still connected, and I know I must be blushing like crazy by now.

"Nice to meet you, Chloe," he says. He stares at me. Am I supposed to say something else? Finally he laughs. "So, you don't want to know my name? I see how it is. Take the jewels and run, huh?"

"No, of course I do. I didn't mean to —" I begin.

"It's Jake," he says. He shakes my hand, and it's only then I realize he is still holding it.

"Nice to meet you, Jake," I mumble, gently pulling my hand away. "And . . . um . . . thanks again."

"Sure. See you on TV," he says with another wink.

I want to say something witty back, but instead I clutch my bag and hurry away.

VARIOUS GOLD CHAINS!

LONG OR SHORT PENDANT?

NECKLACE EMBELLISHMENT *Designs*

CENTER PIECE WITH SMALLER DANGLING PIECES

STUDDED & FACETED WITH CRYSTAL ACCENTS

Celebrity Chloe

Celebrity CHLOE

VINTAGE GOLD STUDS

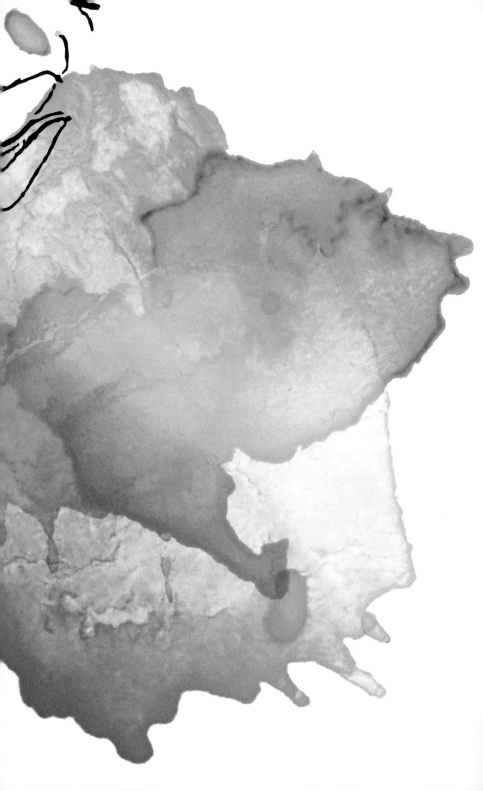

3

It's been two full days since the art fair, and I've pushed all (okay, almost all) thoughts of Jake out of my head in order to focus on my design for the next round of auditions. I've cleared off a section of my floor to use as a workspace and have spread out all the stones and studs Jake gave me. They're even cooler than I initially realized. I have a great assortment of pyramid-shaped, spiked, round, and faceted gold studs to work with. In another pile I've grouped all my findings for the earrings, bracelets, and necklaces — things like clasps, hooks, and earring posts.

Walking in and seeing the mess would probably throw anyone else for a loop, but to me it's complete organization. I have my own system that just works for me. When I was younger, my mom tried to help me clean up, and I couldn't find anything for days. Luckily she gets me now and lets me keep my room in "organized chaos" mode, as she calls it.

This week the plan is eat, sleep, school, create. Rinse, repeat. At least I'm a little less stressed about making jewelry than I am about designing clothes. Maybe it's because it works a different part of my brain or because the patterns are repetitive. I'm not entirely sure what it is, but the process calms me.

I carefully take out the thin beading chain I ordered online and thread some of the larger studs onto it. Then I pick up a small envelope with the most precious stones in my collection of supplies — Swarovski crystals. After I came up with my final design plan, I bought a combination of clear stones in a variety of sizes to add some sparkle to my necklace. I lace the crystals in between Jake's stones to create a pattern.

I move the mannequin over to my window and hold the necklace up against the neckline of the dress. The sun shines on the crystals and the metallic studs are the perfect accent to my neutral dress. The image, offset by the clean, white background, has the exact effect I was hoping for. It elevates the dress from everyday chic to an elegant, formal garment. I continue with the beading patterns, but then stop and inspect it again. It's almost there, but there's something missing.

I add some larger stones and create a pendant necklace, but as soon as I hold it up to the dress I know it's not right. With all the gold tones it looks like some kind of Olympic medal — definitely not what I'm going for. Maybe I need a break. Clearing my mind will probably help.

I set the necklace aside, happy with what I accomplished so far. In fact, it went a lot faster than I thought it would. My stomach picks that moment to growl loudly, reminding me that I haven't eaten since lunch, and it's already six o'clock. I smile, thankful to my parents for not interrupting me while I was working, and head to the kitchen.

"Well, well, well, look who's emerged from the Cave of Style," my dad says with a grin when I walk into the room. "I think it's our daughter . . . at least it looks like her." He makes a big show of squinting and sizing me up like he hasn't seen me in years. "What do you think?" he asks, turning to my mom.

"Hmm," says Mom. She puts her finger on her chin like she's deep in thought and pretends to study me carefully. Sometimes the two of them are so unbelievably dorky together. "Well, it does look like our daughter. But she has this strange look on her face. What would you call that?"

It's like a game of Ping-Pong, and it's now my dad's turn. "Uh, I think they call it happy," he says without missing a beat.

My mom shakes her head and grins. "Oh, then I don't think it's her," she says.

I roll my eyes. If I had a pillow with me, I'd throw it at them. "You guys are so annoying," I say with a laugh.

My dad swipes a hand across his face like he's wiping sweat from his brow. "Phew," he says, "then we're doing something right."

My mom laughs, and I shake my head at their silliness. "Anywaaaay," I drawl, sitting down at the table to join them. "I'm starving."

Dinner looks delicious. The table is fully loaded with all of my favorite foods: spaghetti, turkey meatballs, and my mom's special red sauce. Dad even made garlic bread with three kinds of cheese sprinkled on top — his specialty.

I immediately dig in. All that designing has left me ravenous. "This is so good!" I say between mouthfuls. "Thank you, guys."

"You've been working so hard up there, and we want to make sure we're doing our part in keeping your energy up," Mom replies.

I've really enjoyed making all my designs, but I didn't realize how much I've needed to unwind until this moment. I've been going basically nonstop for the past few weeks, which is what I need for the competition, but taking this break is showing me I need to pause more often. If I make it to New York City, the process will be even more intense. I'll have to remember to make Chloe time so I don't crash and burn. Good thing Mom will be there to watch out for me.

"So when do we get to see your latest and greatest piece?" asks Dad.

"When it's done," I say, smiling. "I want you guys to get the full picture."

"Can you give us any hints?" asks Mom. "Inquiring minds want to know."

I tell them about what I've done so far and my arrangement of studs and crystals.

"That sounds really beautiful," Mom says when I'm finished. "I can't wait to see it."

"Thanks," I tell her. "I really like it so far, but it's just not quite there. It still feels like it's missing something. I'm just not sure what."

"You know," says my dad thoughtfully, "maybe you should take a look at some of the old photo albums we have around the house. I'm not sure where they are, but I seem to remember a lot of your grandpa's old rodeo clown uniforms had really cool, intricate beading. Maybe they'd give you some ideas."

I think back to some outfits I've seen Gramps wear in the pictures. Dad is right — I do remember lots of

embellishments on the outfits. Before he died, we went to a
ceremony to honor him, and I remember a shirt with beading
I liked. I can't remember exactly what it looked like, but I
love Dad's idea, especially considering that the third and final
round of auditions is going to somehow involve the rodeo.
Maybe this will give me a head start if I make it that far.

Dad takes my silence for disagreement. "It was just an
idea," he says. "You don't have to."

"No, no, I was just thinking about it. It's brilliant!" I
tell him. I get out of my chair and round the table to give
him a kiss on the cheek. "Thank you," I tell him gratefully.

Dad grins at me, and I run to the living room. After
digging through a few shelves, I finally find the albums and
start flipping through them. Every time I see something that
I think might work, I make a small sketch and write notes
about the colors. When I get to the third album, I finally see
exactly what I need. If I can pull it off, this design will put
me to the next round for sure.

RODEO INSPIRED *Sketches*

4

"So no one gets to peek under the black cloak of mystery?" asks Alex, nodding to the sheet I've put over my new design. "Not even one teeny tiny peek? Come on!"

I shake my head. There's only one day to go until the next round of auditions, and I guess I've gotten superstitious. I promised my parents and Alex they'll get to see my design tomorrow, and they've tried to be understanding. For the most part, they've succeeded. But being patient? Not so much.

"I told you, I don't want to risk overthinking it," I tell Alex. "Even if you guys say you love it, and it's the most amazing thing ever created —"

"Which I'm sure it will be," Alex interjects.

I can only smile at my best friend's confidence. "Still," I say. "I can see myself explaining it to you guys and then wondering if I should have done something differently."

Alex sighs. "Ugh, I guess you're right," she says. "You do think too much. You need to stop." She throws a pillow across the room at me.

I throw it back. It lands on my nightstand, barely missing a lamp.

"Good thing your dream isn't to play basketball," Alex says with a laugh. She bends to pick up something that fell on the floor. When she holds it up, I realize it's the business card Jake gave me. "Have you looked up this website yet?" she asks.

I shake my head. "I meant to, but I've been so busy creating the necklace and making some tweaks to my dress I just haven't had time."

"You mean to tell me you haven't even thought about hunky Jake?" asks Alex, rolling her eyes. "Come on, Chloe. I'm your best friend. I think I know you better than that."

I feel myself blushing. "Well, I didn't say that. Let's look it up."

Alex opens my laptop and types in the website address for Designs by Liesel. When the website loads, she frowns.

"What's wrong?" I ask.

"There's nothing here except a photo," she says. "The rest of the page just gives the address of her store in New York City and then says 'Under Construction.'"

I lean over to get a better look. "That woman looks so familiar, doesn't she?"

Alex studies the picture. "Probably her eyes," she says. "They look just like Jake's."

"Yeah, but it's more than that," I say, shaking my head. "I know I've seen her somewhere before."

Alex studies the picture again, too. "You're right. She does look really familiar. Maybe she's a regular at art fairs? We could've seen her at one at some point."

I shake my head. "I don't think so. Jake told us that he's the one who usually sells her stuff at the fairs, remember?"

"True," Alex says. "But we've never seen him before either, so you never know."

I keep staring at the computer like if I look long enough the site's 'Under Construction' logo will change into something else. "Oh, well. I give up," I say, closing the laptop.

"You'll have plenty of time to check out her store when you're in New York City," Alex says. "Maybe that will jog your memory."

For once, I don't correct her use of *when* instead of *if*. Instead, I just work on picturing myself in New York City. It's so close I can almost taste it.

5

The next day, my mom, Alex, and I all drive up to San Francisco for the second round of auditions. I lucked out that the *Design Diva* producers decided to hold second round-auditions in both San Francisco and Los Angeles for all the California hopefuls. Los Angeles is at least a five-hour drive from where we live, and I don't know that my parents would have been thrilled about that. Even though there are only seventy contestants left in this round — a major decrease from the hundreds that showed up the first time around — we still get there early.

"I would rather just get it over with right away than keep stressing about it for another ten hours," I say as we walk in.

"I brought my pillow with me this time," Alex says. She sits down and props the pillow against the wall. In minutes, she's breathing deeply and sound asleep.

"Alex could teach us both how to relax," Mom says.

Alex lets out a low snore as if to prove Mom's point. In minutes, the line has already grown behind us. Apparently I'm not the only one who thought it was a good idea to show up early.

From down the hall, I hear Nina whining to her mother. "This is torture," she complains.

"I'm with her," I say to my mom.

My mom raises her eyebrow. "Never thought I'd hear those words," she whispers.

I shrug. "I think since we both made it this far, we have a truce. I don't know if we'll ever be friends, but non-enemies is okay too."

My mom pretends to sniffle and wipe away tears. "My gosh, my little girl is growing up."

I roll my eyes. "You are beyond corny."

Just then, a producer steps out into the hallway. "Chloe Montgomery," she calls. "The judges are ready for you."

I take a deep breath. I thought I'd be less nervous this time, but my palms are sweaty, and the walk to the stage feels longer than ever. I stand under the hot lights and take the black sheet off my necklace and dress.

When I practiced this in my head, the judges gasped in astonishment when they saw my design. A part of me waits for that, but it doesn't happen. Hunter, Missy, and Jasmine look just as serious as ever.

It's just an act, I tell myself. *They have to look that way.* "Should I start?" I ask.

"By all means," says Jasmine.

I try to remember the index cards I made to help me practice so I don't forget anything. I could have brought them with me, but that would have looked unprofessional. I want every little point I can get.

"The last time you saw this dress," I begin, "it was minimalist but fashionable. For this task, I wanted to bring it up a notch. I also wanted to make some changes that help unify the dress with the other designs I made during the last round and create a more cohesive collection. With the added accessories and embellishments, I can see it being worn to a more formal event. And yet it's still not over the top. It has what I like to call a quiet elegance."

I see Jasmine smile at my choice of words. I reviewed some *Design Diva* clips online and found one where Jasmine said she wished more clothing "possessed a quiet elegance." I took it to mean high quality without the loud bling attached, which is exactly what I was going for. From Jasmine's smile, it seems like I hit my mark. I hope that's what the smile means, anyway.

"I used the neutral canvas of my dress as a starting point and played with metallics and crystals to add some modern elegance," I continue. "I also looked back at my other successful design from the first round — the tuxedo leggings and tunic. The leather stripe along the side of the leggings gave me the idea to add leather patches to the shoulders of my bubble dress. The faux leather provides a great contrast to the white of my dress and subtly ties the two pieces together."

Hunter and Missy murmur in agreement, and Jasmine nods her head. Their reaction adds to my confidence. I'm so relieved they seem to like the design as much as I do.

"Very well said, Chloe," Hunter says. "I can see you've put a lot of thought into this. I love that you looked at the bigger picture and referred back to your other designs. The faux leather accents really tie into the leggings you created for the first round of auditions and add a tough edge to what could have been an overly sweet dress. You're already on your way to creating a cohesive collection."

Missy chimes in. "As you probably know from *Design Diva*," she says, "I'm a fan of the bare bones as well. If an outfit has to scream to get my attention, something's not right. The black, white, and metallic color palette you chose just whispers, and it's got me."

"Thank you," I say.

"I can't stop staring at that necklace," says Hunter. "Can you tell us about it?"

"Sure," I reply. "I used a combination of vintage gold studs in different shapes to add dimension and create

THE FIRST CUT

a pattern. The majority of the necklace is studded and faceted pieces with crystal accents. But it still seemed like something was missing. There needed to be a larger statement piece. I made the center piece a circle with smaller pieces dangling from it, like a dream catcher. I think it really ties all the smaller stones together and gives the necklace a focal point."

"That's really unique," Missy says.

Jasmine laughs. "You always say that, Missy," she says, shaking her head. "I don't think anyone even knows what that word means anymore because you say that about everything."

Missy looks hurt, and her face crumples like she's going to cry. "You know what, Jazz? Not everyone has to be nasty for no reason," she snaps.

Jasmine waves her hand dismissively. "I wasn't done. I was going to say that I agree with you for once."

"Well, you could have started with that," Missy mumbles.

It's uncomfortable being up here and watching them fight. I catch Hunter's eye and hope he gets that I need some guidance. He seems to understand, because he clears his throat. "Chloe, the thing that really intrigues me is the pendant in the center. What inspired you to make that?"

Maybe it's the stress of the past few weeks or maybe it's just missing my gramps, but my eyes suddenly fill with tears.

"Oh, good going, Hunter," says Jasmine. "And everyone thinks *I'm* the one who makes people cry."

"No," I say, shaking my head. "It's not his fault." I take a deep breath to collect myself, but when I speak my voice still comes out shaky. "My grandfather was big in the rodeo world. When he was alive, my parents used to take me to see him all the time. When he passed away, we stopped going. I still think about him all the time, though."

I pause and take another breath. "When I was stuck on where to take this necklace, my dad suggested I look at some old photo albums for inspiration. Some of my gramps' rodeo gear had really cool embellishments. I found this photo of him at the rodeo. He looked so happy, like there was no place else he'd rather be. He was wearing this bolo tie around his neck, and it had something that looked like a dream catcher in the middle. That's what inspired me to create this."

When I finish, I wipe tears off my cheeks. I didn't realize how much I missed my gramps, and I feel stupid crying on stage. Good thing I didn't wear make-up today or I'd be a real mess.

"Dang, girl," says Jasmine, "you're making me choke up, too. I don't even have the heart to mess with you. I say definite yes."

"Yes, of course," says Missy.

"Yes, from me too," says Hunter. "But before I give you your next assignment, which, it seems, is a perfect fit for you, I want to give you some advice. What you shared with us just now was gold. Make sure to keep that passion and emotion alive and let it guide you throughout this competition."

I nod, at a loss for words. "Thank you," I finally manage to say.

Hunter hands me the envelope with the next assignment, and I walk off the stage. As soon as I leave the auditorium, I race over to where my mom and Alex are waiting. "I made it to the next round!" I shout, waving the envelope in the air.

"Déjà vu all over again!" yells Alex.

"What's the next assignment?" Mom asks.

"Oh, I haven't even opened it yet." I tear open the envelope and stare at the paper. The words "Rodeo-Inspired Clothing" are printed in big, bold letters.

Hunter wasn't kidding when he said the next challenge would be perfect for me. After my speech about my grandpa, I bet he knew I would love this.

"Awesome!" Alex exclaims, reading over my shoulder.

My mom gives me an excited grin, and I know exactly what she's thinking. Thanks to Gramps, I have this one in the bag.

→ Leather at shoulders!

Fitted Bodice ←

→ Full Gathered Skirt

Pair with Metallic heels!

Neutrals, Black & White, Gold Accents

NECKLACE FINAL Sketches

NECKLACE FINAL *Design*

FINISHED STATEMENT NECKLACE!

BEFORE & AFTER FINAL LOOK

When I get to school the next day, Nina is already waiting for me by my locker. She's alone for once — not a single mini-Nina in sight. This time there are no air kisses or fake hugs, probably because there's no audience there to appreciate them.

Nina holds up an envelope identical to the one Hunter handed me yesterday. "I heard you talking to your mom," she says. "Looks like we're both in the next round."

"Looks like," I say. "It'll be nice to see a familiar face." I never thought I'd say it would be nice to see Nina.

Nina must have been thinking the same thing. "Even if it's me, right?" she says. "Don't worry. I feel the same way."

We both laugh. Nina looks down at her feet like she's not sure what to say. Then, she bends down and takes a small paper bag out of her backpack. "I wanted to give you something," she says, handing me the bag.

Nina is giving me a present? Is the world about to end? "Um, thanks," I say. I stare at the bag, not sure what to do.

"Open it," Nina says.

I do but carefully. I mean, it's Nina. This could be a set-up and live snakes might jump out at any minute.

But when I peek inside, I don't see snakes, rodents, or even bugs. I reach into the bag and pull out a long chain made of gold links. It's so long that it reaches down to my belly button.

To be honest . . . it's kind of ugly. The chain looks bulky and awkward, but I can tell Nina is waiting for me to say something. I don't want to lie and say I love it. I think of how Missy described my necklace. "Wow, thanks, Nina. It's definitely . . . unique," I say.

She grins. "I'm so glad you like it. Can you believe it was only five bucks?"

That much? I think. "What a bargain," I say instead.

"I have on good authority that the judges like this kind of stuff," Nina says, leaning in like she's telling me a secret. "They call it 'out-of-the-box' thinking."

I want to ask her how she knows what the judges want, but I doubt she'd tell me that part. Nina's parents know all sorts of important people, so it's possible she could be telling the truth. "I . . . um . . . I can see how this necklace would fit," I say.

"I got two," Nina replies. "You can even use yours for the next challenge if you want. I might use mine or save it for New York. We'll see. Anyway, this isn't me saying we need to be besties or anything like that." She shrugs and flashes me a smile that looks surprisingly genuine. "I just didn't think it would be fair if I didn't give you a heads-up on what the judges are into. See you later." With a little wave, Nina disappears down the hallway.

"Later," I echo. I put the necklace back in the paper bag and shove it in my backpack. Maybe I will find a use for it, but this challenge won't be the place.

* * *

When I get home that afternoon, I see two trucks parked in front of our house. I take a deep breath and smell food cooking on the grill. My parents didn't say anything about having company, but if it means an impromptu barbecue, bring on the guests.

"There she is, the next *Teen Design Diva!*" says my dad as I walk up. "Watch out, celebrity coming through."

For a change, I decide to play along with the attention and curtsy. "Autographs, anyone? I won't even charge you this time. Friends and family discount," I say with a wink.

Everyone laughs. Seated at the table with my mom are two of Gramps's best buddies, Jim and George. We haven't seen them in at least a year. I hurry over and hug them both hello. "What are you guys doing here?" I ask.

"We came to help," Jim replies. "Your dad tells us you have a rodeo-inspired challenge coming up, and there's nothing we like more than talking about the good old days, right, George?"

"That's right," says George, running a hand through his gray hair. "Hopefully our stories can give you some ideas for your designs."

"Rodeo has changed a lot through the years," Jim says. "For the better, I'd say. Back when your granddaddy and I were boys, there were no helmets. Nowadays, they encourage them."

"I don't do much riding these days, but I sure wish they'd required them back in our time. Hit my head so many times, my memory ain't what it used to be," says George.

My dad flips over the meat on the grill, and it sizzles. "Maybe you can do something with that, Chloe," he suggests. "Embellish the helmets to make them look cooler."

Somehow I don't think embellished helmets are *exactly* what the judges are looking for. Based on the challenge description, it seems like our designs should be more rodeo-inspired than recreations of actual rodeo gear. Plus, I can't imagine macho rodeo guys being psyched to wear a helmet covered in jewels and other embellishments. And even if they were into it, I don't have much experience with headgear. Now is not the time to experiment.

Before I can figure out a way to decline, Mom speaks up. "What about the clothing itself?" she says, shooting me a look. "I think that's more Chloe's strength, right, hon?"

I can always count on my mom to be on the same page as me. "That's true," I say, apologetically. I glance over at my dad, hoping I didn't hurt his feelings too much.

He moves the steak to a plate and drizzles it with sauce. "You do what you think is best, Chloe," he says, smiling. "I'm not all caught up on my *GQ* yet."

I smile. I doubt my dad will ever be fashion-forward, but it's nice of him to try.

"Bring that bad boy right over here," Jim says, getting his fork and knife ready to dive into the steak.

Dad takes another steak off the grill and brings both to the table. Good thing they both were ready at the same time or there might have been a rodeo brawl in our backyard, bull not included.

Jim and George dig into their steaks while Mom and I wait for dad's special blue-cheese burgers. Suddenly, George's eyes light up, and he takes a swig of his lemonade to wash down his food so he can speak. "How about colors?" he suggests. "Our riding gear could certainly use some."

"It's not a fashion show, George. People come to watch the sport," Jim says.

George turns on him. "It *is* a fashion show now, Jimmy, remember?"

Jim's face reddens. "Sorry, Chloe, I forgot," he says apologetically. "I'm a little old school. George is right. Color could sure liven things up."

I can't help but laugh at his discomfort. "No worries, Jim. You're right — it is about the sport. But, there are probably fans who come to show off their latest gear, too. So, for them, the costume change would be something different."

An idea begins to brew in my head. I think about the current color palette of tans and neutrals and ways to liven it up. I don't want anything too crazy, but some brighter colors and cool embellishments — fringe, studs, grommets, things like that — could make it more fashionable.

My parents continue to laugh with Gramps's friends, but I take my burger and excuse myself to check out Gramps's albums again. I never thought I'd find myself designing rodeo clothing, but after talking to Jim and George I'm feeling inspired. I want to make those outfits so hot that the judges won't know what hit them.

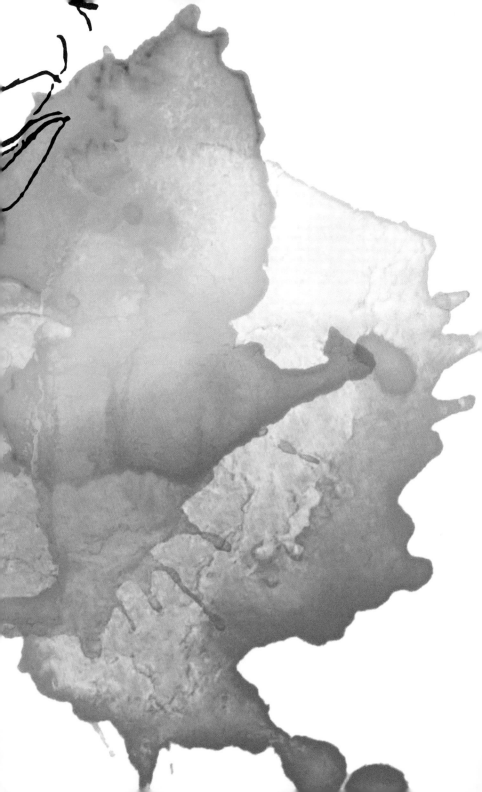

7

I spend the next few days looking at old photos, researching everything I can find about rodeo attire, and trying to get my design plan just right. This challenge is a little unconventional — not entirely surprising since *Design Diva* loves throwing the unexpected at contestants to see how well they can think outside the box. And rodeo-inspired clothing is *definitely* outside the box.

George was onto something when he mentioned embellishments. Rodeo gear is usually suede or leather chaps worn over jeans and paired with a button-down shirt. It's a functional combination for riders . . . but it's not exactly a fashionable one. Still, I know it's important to respect the tradition of rodeo *and* incorporate the judges' theme, so I'm sticking with the somewhat traditional color scheme of brown, blue, gold, and tan. Then I'll spice up the outfit with cool embellishments.

My rodeo-inspired ensemble will feature a much slimmer, more feminine silhouette than the usual uniform. I'm creating a pair of slim, bootcut jeans accented with studded leather fringe. Instead of a traditional button-down shirt, I'm making a fitted vest with a cinched waist.

It was really nice having Gramps's friends here, relaxing and telling stories. It's been a long time since we were that happy while talking about him. At least for me. It's hard to talk about him without missing him. But right now, I try to keep my focus on the happy. I have all my materials spread out in front me — denim for my jeans, several yards of blue plaid for my vest, and all my embellishments.

Today Alex has come over to watch me work. She's lying on her stomach on my bedroom floor and has her math homework spread out in front of her. She does a problem, then watches me work. Problem, then watch. Back and forth, back and forth, and it's making me anxious.

Finally I sigh loudly. "Stop!" I say.

"I'm sorry, I can't help it!" Alex says. "I just want to see what kind of progress you're making. Besides, watching you is way more interesting than studying algebra."

I immediately feel bad for snapping at her. "Yeah, I get it," I say. "I'm sorry. I'm just a little stressed. This has to be perfect."

Alex makes a big show of oohing and ahhing over what I've done so far. But as she moves around my mess of supplies, she bumps into a can of soda that she's placed precariously close to my pile of fabric. Luckily, she grabs it before it can spill. "Sorry," she says.

"If you had actually spilled it, you'd really be sorry," I say through gritted teeth.

"Tough girl is an interesting look for you," she says, cocking her head like she's examining me. "I can call you Cranky Chloe, or —"

"Alex!" I snap.

Alex sighs. "I need something to do," she says. "I feel so useless."

"You have a math test tomorrow," I tell her. "Study." I know it's mostly due to the stress of the competition, but I'm starting to get annoyed with her. I definitely don't want Alex to be a casualty of my wrath. "Maybe you should go."

"You need me to save you from yourself, Cranky Chloe," she says as she opens my laptop. She's probably looking up synonyms for cranky that start with C so she can add to my CC nickname. Whatever. As long as she's quiet it doesn't matter to me. I love my best friend, but when I'm working, I need to focus.

I figure out the measurements I'll need for the waist and inseam of my jeans and jot them down on my sketchpad. Then I do the same with the measurements for the thighs, knees, and calves. I want to make sure I have everything correct.

Measure twice, cut once — that's what Mimi, the owner of my favorite fabric and vintage store, always says.

Once the jeans are finished, I'm planning to add some studded leather fringe along the outside seams. That will be the perfect modern twist on traditional riding chaps.

To contrast with the dark denim bottoms, I've chosen a bright blue plaid for my vest. As I was studying traditional rodeo gear, the one thing that really stood out to me was how boxy and unflattering the button-down shirts are. I mean, I don't love skintight tops, but I want my vest to have some definition. Figure-flattering and feminine, that's what I'm going for. The updated silhouette done in a more traditional fabric is the perfect combination for this challenge. (I just hope the judges agree!)

I settled on a flattering deep V-neck for the vest, which will be much more elongating on whomever is wearing it, and I'm using cool brass buttons on the front. They remind me of the metal embellishments on the horses' saddles and bridles, which is exactly what I'm going for. I want this to be an elegant take on rodeo-inspired fashion. Not a costume.

I spend the entire afternoon sewing. By the time I take a break, my shoulders ache from hunching over my sewing machine. I hang what I have so far on my dress form and mentally play around with some different Western accessories.

Maybe it needs a belt or something, I think, studying my creation. *Or maybe cowboy boots.* At this point, my brain is exhausted, and I need a break. I don't want to overdo the embellishments.

"Can I help with anything?" Alex asks.

I glance over at her and rack my brain, trying to remember the last time I thanked her for all her help and for putting up with my mood swings lately. Without answering, I get up and go hug her.

Alex is clearly startled. "What gives? Is someone dying?" she asks.

"No, nothing like that. I just realized you're the best friend ever, and I don't think I tell you that enough at all," I say.

Alex shrugs. "Aw, girl," she says in a silly voice. "You're going to make me cry." She grins and goes back to her homework, but I swear she wipes at her eyes with the back of her hand.

8

By the time Saturday finally rolls around, I'm so nervous I can hardly stand still. I barely slept the night before. I kept having nightmares about embarrassing myself in front of the judges and the entire audience. In one particularly vivid dream, I was standing on the rodeo stage, and just as I was in the middle of explaining my color scheme, I fell right into the judges, who just happened to be eating pie. Come one and all, and witness the spectacle that is Clumsy Chloe.

My mom, dad, Alex, and I all pile into our car and drive the forty-five minutes to the rodeo grounds in Salinas. When we arrive, the place is already packed with camera crews, booths, food, and rides. This is not typical for June in Salinas. The massive California Rodeo isn't held until the third week in July. There are parades, kids' events, and fairs that take place in the two weeks before that. Basically, July is one big funfest. But this special event to promote *Teen Design Diva* has really drawn a crowd. I guess I shouldn't be surprised — northern Cali does love its cowboys, and everyone seems happy to start the festivities early.

"It's like an appetizer until the real thing comes along. What's not to like about that?" I heard George say the other day.

Just then our car pulls into a parking spot. Everyone climbs out, and I spot George and Jim waiting for us by the entrance.

"Today's your big day," says Alex, giving my arm a squeeze. "This is so exciting! Look how many people are already here!"

Alex is right. This will be a much bigger crowd than I faced in the past two rounds. Not that I wasn't nervous during both of those rounds, but at least then it was just me in front of the three judges. I know she's trying to be encouraging, but suddenly I feel sick. I'm hot. I'm cold. My stomach is doing its own version of riding the bronco, and I close my eyes and swallow to stop my breakfast from coming up.

The rodeo is not normally my big day. It belongs to the riders and food vendors and Miss Rodeo California.

When I was a kid, I wanted more than anything to be Miss Rodeo. That was until I realized I'm more the design-the-outfits-for-the-pageant type than the beauty-queen type.

Alex must be thinking the same thing because she says, "Hey! You finally get to be queen for the day!"

The thought of everyone watching me as I try to explain my rodeo-inspired designs to the judges, plus hundreds of other people, almost turns throwing up from an idea into a reality. I quickly lean over and put my head between my knees, taking deep breaths to try and settle my stomach. I'm really hoping I don't puke all over my favorite boots.

My dad rubs my back, and my mom pulls my hair away from the line of fire just in case. I don't have to look to know that Alex is as far away as possible, trying to focus on anything else. Just the mention of someone throwing up turns her face green.

Thankfully, I manage to avoid actually puking and embarrassing myself, and when I've recovered, we all walk to the entrance. A reporter approaches us, but my dad intercepts him and whispers something. The reporter nods and says he'll come back later. I can picture the headline now: "Chloe Montgomery: Sick with Excitement."

When we reach the entrance to the rodeo grounds,I see Jim, George, and some of my grandpa's other buddies waiting for us. They immediately surround me, big smiles on their faces.

"We can't wait to see what Chloe cooked up for today," George says.

"Speaking of cooking," Jim pipes up, "some of the best baked beans and sausage I've ever eaten are under that canopy over there. Can I convince anyone to check it out with me?" He points to the Vendors' Row.

My stomach gives another little lurch at the mention of food, but the smells around me are so inviting, I can't resist following Jim. Some of my usual favorites, like calamari, Philly cheesesteak sandwiches, and Louisiana gumbo call to me, but I decide to start small with kettle corn, cotton candy, and lemonade and save the rest for after my on-stage presentation. Nothing like sugar to calm the nerves.

I bring my food to a bench and take small bites while Alex investigates the rest of the food booths. From my spot, I can see more *Teen Design Diva* contestants arriving and exploring the fair too.

Suddenly a shadow falls over me. "Looks like quite the healthy breakfast you have there," a guy's voice says.

I know that voice, and so do my palms because they immediately start sweating. I glance up and see Jake grinning down at me.

Salinas
RODEO
PHOTOS

FERRIS WHEEL

COTTON CANDY

TICKETS

COTTON CANDY!!!

✓ COTTON CANDY
✓ KETTLE CORN
✓ LEMONADE

Cowboy Boots:
Fair Attire

What's he doing here? I wonder. But then he sits down beside me, and I lose my train of thought. I notice he has a big slice of cherry pie on his plate. "You too," I say, nodding at his choice of food.

"Yup," Jake says with a grin. "Got my whole grains and fruit, and I bet the crust was made with eggs, so I'm counting that as a protein."

I look down at my food to see how to spin it. "Fruit!" I say, pointing to my lemonade. "Oh, and corn is a vegetable. We're such health nuts."

Jake laughs. "Hey, I like your necklace," he says, nodding toward my chest.

I put my hand up to my throat. I'd totally forgotten that I was wearing the necklace he gave me at the art fair. I figured it might bring me some much-needed luck today.

"Thanks," I say, blushing a little. "By the way, the stones I got from you worked perfectly in my design. Got me to this last round."

Jake smiles, and his dimples make another brief appearance. "That's so awesome," he says. "One to go then, right?"

"Yep," I say. "Oh, look! They're starting to display some of the designs."

I point toward the stage where producers are busy setting up jewelry, boots, and other rodeo-inspired gear for the big presentation. Some of the designs have a lot of embellishments on them — fringe, beading, bright colors, you name it. Others are more muted looking, done in tans and neutrals.

"Which one's yours?" Jake asks.

"The one at the end," I tell him, pointing to where a producer is working on displaying my plaid vest and fringed jeans.

Jake studies the pieces for a moment but doesn't say anything.

"Not your style?" I ask.

He shakes his head. "No, that's not it at all. I was just trying to think of a way to describe it, like they teach us in marketing. I like it a lot. My mom will too. It's a really modern take on rodeo."

"Speaking of your mom, I tried looking up her website, but it didn't work," I tell him. "She looked really familiar, though."

"Do you want to meet her?" Jake asks. "She's here, and I bet she'd be really excited to hear about how her designs helped you."

"Sure!" I agree. I quickly wipe the cotton candy from mouth and hope I look presentable."Bring it on."

9

As Jake leads me across the fairgrounds, I see Alex examining some clothes on a vendor's table and motion to her to come along too. As soon as she realizes who I'm walking with, her eyes grow huge, and she immediately hurries over.

"You have to spill later," Alex whispers in my ear. Thankfully, she leaves it at that and doesn't nudge Jake or ask anything embarrassing.

Suddenly, I see her — Lisa McKay, the season three winner of *Design Diva*. She was one of the few designers who really made it big after the show. Not only is her clothing line amazing, but she also has her own line of jewelry now.

"Oh my gosh," I squeal, grabbing Alex. "It's her!"

Alex may not be much for fashion, but she's as big a fan of the show as I am, and immediately realizes who I'm talking about. "OMG!" she echoes, grabbing my hand. "Lisa McKay!"

Out of the corner of my eye, I see Jake biting his lip like he's trying not to laugh at us. Whatever. I don't care if he thinks we're acting like silly groupies. It's Lisa McKay!

"I know her," says Jake. "I can introduce you guys if you want."

My eyes bug out, and Alex and I can't do anything but nod and follow him. In seconds, we're standing next to Lisa McKay's table, and I'm too starstruck to say a word.

"Hi there, girls," says Lisa, extending her hand. She's so calm and sweet and not unnerved at all by our gawking. She's probably used to silly fangirls by now. I'm sure people approach her all the time.

"Um, hi," I manage to say. I look to Alex for help, but she seems to be at a loss for words for once.

Jake looks at us, waiting for us to say more, and when he sees we won't, he takes matters into his own hands. "Mom, this is Chloe, the girl I was telling you about. The one who was really into your designs. And this is her friend Alex."

Just then, Jake's words penetrate my starstruck brain. *Mom?* I think.

Suddenly I realize why I didn't recognize Lisa from her website. In the photo online, her hair is super short and spiky. Now, it's past her shoulders and wavy, just like it was on the show.

Alex finally pipes up and points out the other thing that was confusing me. "But your card says Liesel," she says, clearly just as confused as I am.

Jake's mother chuckles. "That's because Liesel is my name. The producers kept getting it wrong on the show, and after a while I just gave up and stopped correcting them," she says with a shrug. "I mean, who cares what they call me as long as I win, right?"

"I owe you big time," I say, finally finding my voice. "Well, you and Jake both. Your pieces really put my last design over the top in the last round of auditions. Thank you so much."

Liesel waves her hand like it's nothing. "I can't wait to see what you did with them. Oh!" She looks at my necklace, just noticing it. "That looks stunning on you! And to think I wanted to chuck it. Shows what I know."

Just then, the static of a microphone interrupts our conversation. We all turn toward the stage and see Jasmine standing there, waiting for quiet. "Designers, we'll be starting in five minutes," she announces. "Please take your seats at the front of the stage."

I let out a nervous, shuddering breath. "That's me," I say. "It was so nice to meet you."

"You too, sweetie," Liesel says with a smile. "Knock 'em dead."

"Good luck," Jake adds. "You'll be great."

Alex and I walk toward the stage, and she squeezes my hand tightly. "You're going to be great," she says. "I know it. Just remember to be confident. Your designs rock."

I take a seat with the rest of the design hopefuls and see that Nina is already there. She's the only one I recognize, which isn't that surprising since the contestants have come from all over. We nod at each other. I can tell she's nervous too.

When all the designers are finally seated, Jasmine makes her way back up to the stage and picks up the microphone again. "Welcome, everyone, to the final round of *Teen Design Diva* auditions," she starts. "Let me begin by saying what an honor it is to be here. I know many of you were probably surprised when you found out about the nature of this challenge. After all, rodeo clothing isn't usually something you'd see featured on Rodeo Drive."

Jasmine pauses, and the audience laughs at her pun. "However, being a successful designer means being versatile, and that's something we want our teen designers to learn early on. If you want to win this competition, you must be ready to tackle any challenge — no matter how unique. And just like a fashion show, rodeo is a performance. There's an art to it. I hope the forty designs we see today do justice to that."

I like how Jasmine phrases that, combining the beauty of designing and the rodeo. I make circles in the dirt with my boots, waiting for the competition to begin. Finally, it's time. The stands fall silent as the first designer takes the stage.

First up is a girl named Daphne Corral. A burst of nervous laughter escapes me as I think about her last name. Corral, rodeo — maybe it's a sign. Her design involves embellishing the existing uniforms with studs, beading, and small gems. It's not the route I would have thought to take, but her result is pretty amazing. She chose earthy tones and used bright blues as accents. At the end, she even makes a joke about her last name, and the crowd laughs.

The next contestant, whose name I don't catch, freezes onstage. I can totally sympathize with how she's feeling. When she finally speaks, she describes the mauve she chose as periwinkle and gets flustered. Missy tries to talk soothingly to her, but it doesn't seem to help much. In the end, Hunter has to explain most of her pieces, but it's clear he doesn't get exactly what she was going for.

One by one, more designers take the stage, and the crowd filters in and out. It takes a long time to go through

OTHER CONTESTANTS' *Designs*

DAPHNE'S LOOK
RODEO INSPIRED

NINA'S LOOK
RODEO INSPIRED

forty designs, but the contestants and their families don't move. We all want to see the competition. Some of the designs I like, others I don't, but it's hard to tell which direction the judges will lean. Everyone's taste is so different. That was obvious the night Jim and George came over.

Soon, it's Nina's turn. Even though she seemed nervous before, you can't tell from her confident strut to the stage. Nina chose to change the color of the traditional rodeo clothing and used shades of green in her design. The judges ask her about her color choices, and she says she focused on greens because she wanted "to be one with nature." That's so not Nina, but I doubt anyone will know or care. All that matters is how the designs look, and even though it pains me to admit it, hers is one of my favorites.

Finally, there's only one designer left before it'll be my turn — a guy named Derek Bonnell. Derek walks easily and confidently to the stage, but he doesn't strut like Nina did. When the judges ask, he explains that he chose to focus on the boots for his design, which is not an easy task. I love to buy shoes, but I definitely don't attempt to make them.

Derek continues talking about how he dyed the leather and stitched the looped design on the side of the boots. He also did something to the sole of the boot to add traction.

OTHER CONTESTANTS' *Designs*

Simple sweetheart neckline dress

Belt:
leather with
stud trim
(match boots)

Colors:
tan/pink/gold

Boots: suede and
leather with stud trim
- Handpainted
Roses on sides
and on toe bed

DEREK'S LOOK
RODEO INSPIRED

Derek's functional alteration gets some approving buzz from the rodeo riders in the audience. Up until now, the designs have focused on the aesthetics, not anything functional.

It's amazing to be a part of this and witness so much talent, but to be honest, I'm getting a little discouraged. I like my designs, but there are *so* many good ones here. What sets each one apart? What is that one thing that will make the judges choose mine?

"Thank you so much, Derek," Jasmine says. "We have one design left to go. Let's welcome Chloe Montgomery to the stage."

I smile and don't realize I'm not moving until my mom leans forward and gently nudges me. I don't remember walking to the stage, yet suddenly, I find myself looking out into hundreds of faces. The sun beats down on my skin, and I clear my throat.

Speak, Chloe, speak! I think frantically.

Suddenly I see Jake give me a small wave from the audience. I see my parents and Alex smiling and giving me encouraging thumbs-up signals. I take a deep breath. Confident Chloe is back. I can do this.

Missy smiles at me. "It's nice to see you again, Chloe," she begins. "Why don't you tell us a little bit about the rodeo-inspired design you created for today."

I've answered this question about all my other designs so far, so I'm ready with an answer. "I think the rodeo attire used today serves a purpose, but from what I've heard from some of the riders, the uniform could use some spicing up," I begin. Who cares if *some* was really *one*? There have to be others who agree. Whoops come from the audience, so apparently there are.

"My grandpa was really involved in rodeo, so when I was planning my design, I wanted to create something that spoke to the tradition of that but also added a modern twist," I continue. "That's why I decided to use a more traditional color palette but opted for something with a slimmer silhouette. I also added studs and fringe to embellish the outfit."

Jasmine nods. "Why did you decide to add the studs and the fringe?" she asks. "Did you not think the jeans were enough on their own?"

This question throws me off, and I try to read Jasmine's expression. Is she purposely trying to stump me or does she really hate my idea? I must focus on her a little too long because I see the audience shifting and getting restless.

I sigh. Who knows what Jasmine is really thinking? I'll just answer honestly. "Actually, I toyed around with several different ideas," I say. "I didn't want to use too many embellishments because I wanted my design to be wearable — not a costume. I think the fringe and the studs provide the perfect balance. They're interesting without being too over-the-top."

Hunter leans forward in his seat. "What I like about this is the comfort you've shown with embellishments. I mean, from what you told us previously, that's not usually your thing, right?"

I hear my family and Alex laugh in the audience. "That's definitely true," I say, smiling, "but the rodeo is different. It's massive. It deserves a little flash and sparkle."

RODEO FINAL *Design*

FITTED VEST

CINCHED WAIST

LEATHER STUDDED FRINGE

SLIM, BOOTCUT JEANS

Color Palette:
Browns, Blues,
& Plaid

"Thank you so much, Chloe," Missy says as the crowd applauds and whistles. "We'll take a short break as we discuss all these wonderful designs, and we'll then announce who will be continuing on to the competition in New York."

I walk back to my seat, feeling good. I did my best. Now all I can do is wait.

* * *

An hour later, I'm starting to realize that waiting is easier said than done. I explore the booths to pass some time, and I even manage to down some gumbo, which is just as fantastic and spicy as it has been in the past. But as good as the food is, it can't distract me for long, and I end up making my way back to my front-row seat to wait.

Once I'm seated, I look around at the other contestants. Everyone tried so hard, but only fifteen of us will make it to New York City. It's not easy having that next step be so close, only to have it fall through. I clench my hands into tight fists as if that can stop the win from slipping through my fingers.

Just then, Jake slides into the open seat next to me. "You were fantastic up there," he says encouragingly. "My mom thought so too. You really held your own with the judges — especially Jasmine. She's tough."

It's great to hear that Jake liked what I had to say, but knowing that Liesel McKay liked my designs is really amazing. Assuming Jake didn't just say that to make me feel good, that is. "Thanks," I reply. "That means a lot."

"Someone told me that Garrett Montgomery was your grandpa," Jake says, impressed. "I didn't know that."

I shrug. "I didn't realize you followed the rodeo," I tell him.

"My dad is big on the scene," Jake says. He points to a man in the crowd, but I don't recognize him. Then again, I really only know Gramps' friends, and Jake's dad is on the young side. "I've been hearing about your grandpa since I was in diapers. He seemed like a good guy."

"He was," I say. "Thinking about him helped motivate me to get here." I look to the stage and see no judges. "It's been more than an hour. I wonder how close they are to making decisions."

Jake nods to the side of the stage, and I spot Missy walking toward the microphone. "I think they're about to tell us," he says.

Everyone else must have been scoping out the stage too, because the crowd quiets down before Missy even has a chance to speak.

"Usually, we drag things out far longer," Missy starts, "but there are some delicious-looking sandwiches and pie calling my name."

The crowd laughs. "Don't forget the sausage and gumbo!" someone shouts.

"Oh, I won't, sugar," Missy says. "This belly is starved." There's more laughter, and Missy waits for quiet before she continues. "First I want to say that this was not an easy decision. We have forty very talented designers here, and it would be wonderful to see every rodeo rider in one of their designs, but unfortunately, we can't do that. The lucky fifteen we choose, however, will see their designs displayed proudly at the California Rodeo next month. So without further ado, Hunter and Jasmine will read the names of the designers who will be going to New York City to continue their quest for the fashion internship."

Jasmine and Hunter walk onstage, each carrying a list of names with them, and begin to read them off. The crowd cheers for each one, and the winners run to the stage. Derek and Daphne are both called, and halfway through the list, I hear Nina's name. The list continues, and I'm counting the numbers — they're up to fourteen designers now. I can't even figure out the order. It's definitely not alphabetical, or I'd have been after Nina.

"One more name, ladies and gentlemen. My apologies to Missy and her stomach, but we're going to drag this out a little more here," Hunter says.

Missy clutches her stomach and looks longingly at the food vendors.

"The last contestant going to New York City gave me some pause in the beginning," Jasmine tells the crowd.

"That could be anyone," I mumble.

"She's had some highs and lows," Jasmine continues, building the suspense.

Hunter grabs the mic away. "One low, Jazz, not some," he corrects her.

Jasmine rolls her eyes. "I'm trying to add some suspense. Anyway, she's had many more highs than lows. How's that?"

"Much better," Hunter says. "This designer really touched us with her family story."

At that, I perk up. That could be me! Hunter told me they liked me talking from the heart. I feel my mom's hand squeeze my shoulder from behind.

"Oh, for heaven's sake," says Missy, taking the microphone. "I can't stand it. She's from right here in California."

When she says this, the crowd goes wild. I glance behind me and see my family and Alex jumping up and down. What if there's someone else from California? I desperately try to remember if there's anyone else besides Nina and me.

"Chloe Montgomery!" the judges shout in unison. "Come on up here!"

OMG.

I can't believe it! Did they really just say my name? I feel like I'm in a daze, and then someone's hand is on my back, pushing me forward. I run to the stage and find myself engulfed in a hug with all the other contestants and judges. I feel like I'm dreaming and have to resist the urge to pinch myself. Am I really going to New York?!

Cameras are in our faces, and the reporters surrounding the stage are shouting questions at us. How do we feel? Did we have a feeling we'd be the final fifteen? What do we think about New York City? Everyone is talking at once, and the reporters try to get all our names down.

"Nina and Chloe," one reporter shouts, "we've been following your story from the beginning. Now both of you are headed to New York City. Is there really no rivalry between you girls?"

I open my mouth to say it will be nice to see a familiar face in New York, but before I can get a word out, Nina jumps in and cuts me off. "I guess time will tell, right?" she says.

The reporter raises his eyebrows. "Interesting. And you, Chloe, what do you want to say about your journey?"

There's so much to say, I don't even know where to start. "It's been incredible," I say. "I've learned I'm capable of much more than I thought and to not let things stand in the way of my dream." That sounds a little cheesy and rehearsed, but it's true.

"Well said," the reporter replies, eating up my words of wisdom. "Now let's get a photo of our Santa Cruz girls."

Nina looks wary, but when a photographer steps forward, she puts her arm around me and pastes a smile on her face. When the flash goes off, I'm grinning from ear to ear. Who cares if I'm hugging Nina? I made it. New York City, here I come!

Keep reading for a sneak

peek of the next book in the

CHLOE *by* **DESIGN** series:

UNRAVELING

I can't believe it. I'm finally here. New York City.

Everything has been a total whirlwind since the last round of auditions. I packed my bags, and my mom and I headed to New York City for the remainder of the competition.

There's so much energy and craziness everywhere. The city is all taxis honking, people yelling, and lights flashing. It's different and scary, but thrilling too.

I look around our hotel lobby, the meeting place for the *Teen Design Diva* orientation. The letter delivered to my hotel room said all fifteen contestants should meet here. Everything looks so elegant — the marble floors, the plants hugging each corner of the room, and the soft, beige leather chairs. The other contestants are gathered nearby, and I recognize a few people from the earlier rounds of auditions, but the only person I really know is Nina. Given our history, I'm not exactly anxious to go talk to her. I wonder if everyone else is feeling just as nervous and excited as I am.

Just then, the elevator doors whoosh open, and Missy, Jasmine, and Hunter walk into the lobby. They're followed by a camera crew. Even though I've met them in person multiple times now, my heart still starts to race at the sight of them.

Missy smiles warmly at all the contestants. "First of all, we'd like to welcome all of our talented designers to the Big Apple. Even if you're from New York City or have been here before, I guarantee this competition will be like no other experience you've ever had. When things get tough, remember to keep your eye on the prize — an internship with one of the city's top designers. It's an opportunity every designer dreams of, and it could be yours." With that, Missy waves Jasmine forward.

Jasmine's stilettos click on the floor, all business, as she steps to the front. "Let's get the important stuff out of the way. As I'm sure you already know, you'll be in New York for one month. There will be a total of seven challenges, and two contestants will be eliminated after each challenge. The show will be taped, except for the final elimination, which will air live. All the challenges will be timed, and unless stated otherwise, you will be allowed to use only the materials we supply." Jasmine turns to Hunter. "Anything else you want to add?"

"Be creative," Hunter says, smiling at the group. "Use your strengths, but don't be afraid to try something new. Think outside the box."

At this last suggestion, I feel a poke in my back. I can't be sure, but it's probably Nina saying I told you so. That's exactly what she said the judges were looking for when she gave me that weird necklace back home. Looks like she was just being nice after all.

"And remember," Missy adds, "have fun!"

"Your first challenge will be held tomorrow morning at nine o'clock in the Central Park Zoo," Jasmine tells us. "Your packets have maps as well as walking and subway directions. Don't be late."

MARGIE

Author Bio

Margaret Gurevich has wanted to be a writer since second grade. She has written for many magazines and currently writes young adult and middle grade books. She loves hiking, cooking, reading, watching too much television, and spending time with her husband and son.

BROOKE

Illustrator Bio

Brooke Hagel is a fashion illustrator based in New York City. While studying fashion design at the Fashion Institute of Technology, she began her career as an intern, working in the wardrobe department of *Sex and the City*, the design studios of Cynthia Rowley, and the production offices of *Saturday Night Live*. After graduating, Brooke began designing and styling for Hearst Magazines, contributing to *Harper's Bazaar*, *House Beautiful*, *Seventeen*, and *Esquire*. Brooke is now a successful illustrator with clients including *Vogue*, *Teen Vogue*, *InStyle*, Dior, Brian Atwood, Hugo Boss, Barbie, Gap, and Neutrogena.

MEASURE TWICE, CUT ONCE
OR YOU WON'T
MAKE THE
Cut

CHLOE *by* DESIGN

DESIGN *Diva*

THE FIRST *Cut*

*Un*RAVELING

DESIGN *Destiny*

BY MARGARET GUREVICH · ILLUSTRATED BY BROOKE HAGEL

READ THEM ALL!